ISBN 1 85534 586 2

Printed and bound in Slovenia.

Chicken-Licken

Retold by Judy Hamilton
Illustrated by R. James Binnie

Tarantula Books

Once upon a time there was a little chicken called Chicken-Licken, who lived in the farmyard by the woods. Chicken-Licken was young and not very clever. One fine autumn day, as Chicken-Licken was scratching about under the trees at the edge of the woods, an acorn fell from a tree and landed on Chicken-Licken's head.

"Ouch!" said Chicken-Licken. "What was that?"

Then Chicken-Licken gasped in horror.

"Oh, my goodness!" he cried. "It must have been a piece of the sky! I must go and tell the king about this!"

So Chicken-Licken scurried off into the woods in search of the king, to tell him that the sky was falling to earth.

As Chicken-Licken ran through the woods, he came across Henny-Penny, clucking quietly among the trees. She was very surprised to see Chicken-Licken.

"My goodness, Chicken-Licken," she said, "why are you so far from home and why do you look so worried?"

"A piece of the sky came down upon my head!" cried Chicken-Licken. "I am going to tell the king about it!"

"How terrible!" said Henny-Penny. "Let me come with you!"

So Chicken-Licken and Henny-Penny scurried off together to tell the king that the sky was falling to earth.

Further into the woods, Chicken-Licken and Henny-Penny met Cocky-Locky. He was very-surprised to see them.

"My goodness, Chicken-Licken," he said, "why are you so far from home and why do you look so worried?"

"A piece of the sky came down upon my head!" cried Chicken-Licken. "We are going to tell the king about it!"

"How terrible!" said Cocky-Locky. "Let me come with you!"

So Chicken-Licken, Henny-Penny and Cocky-Locky scurried off together to tell the king that the sky was falling to earth.

As they came towards the duckpond, Chicken-Licken, Henny-Penny and Cocky-Locky met Ducky-Lucky. She was very surprised to see them.

"My goodness, Chicken-Licken," she said, "why are you all so far from home and why do you look so worried?"

"A piece of the sky fell down upon my head!" cried Chicken-Licken. "We are going to tell the kin about it!"

"How terrible!" said Ducky-Lucky. "Let me com with you!"

So Chicken-Licken, Henny-Penny, Cocky-Locky and Ducky-Lucky scurried off together to tell the king that the sky was falling to earth.

As they reached the far side of the duckpond, Chicken-Licken, Henny-Penny, Cocky-Locky and Ducky-Lucky met Drakey-Lakey. He was very surprised to see them.

"My goodness, Chicken-Licken," he said, "why are you all so far from home and why do you look so worried?"

"A piece of the sky came down upon my head!" cried Chicken-Licken. "We are going to tell the king about it!"

"How terrible!" said Drakey-Lakey. "Let me come with you!"

So Chicken-Licken, Henny-Penny, Cocky-Locky, Ducky-Lucky and Drakey-Lakey scurried off together to tell the king that the sky was falling to earth.

To tell the truth, Chicken-Licken, Henny-Penny, Cocky-Locky, Ducky-Lucky and Drakey-Lakey were all rather foolish birds. Not one of them knew where to find the king, and not one of them thought to ask. They all scurried on as fast as their little legs would carry them without a single idea about where, exactly, they were going. They ran across the field together and when they got near the other side, they met Goosey-Loosey. She was very surprised to see them.

"My goodness, Chicken-Licken," she said, "why are you all so far from home and why do you look so worried?"

"A piece of the sky came down upon my head!" cried Chicken-Licken. "We are going to tell the king about it!"

"How terrible!" said Goosey-Loosey. "Let me come with you!"

So Chicken-Licken, Henny-Penny, Cocky-Locky, Ducky-Lucky, Drakey-Lakey and Goosey-Loosey scurried off together to tell the king that the sky was falling to earth.

They had not gone much further when they met Gander-Lander. He was very surprised to see them.

"My goodness, Chicken-Licken," he said, "Why are you all so far from home and why do you look so worried?"

"A piece of the sky came down upon my head!" cried Chicken-Licken. "We are going to tell the king about it!"

"How terrible!" said Gander-Lander. "Let me come with you!"

So Chicken-Licken, Henny-Penny, Cocky-Locky, Ducky-Lucky, Drakey-Lakey, Goosey-Loosey and Gander-Lander scurried off together to tell the king that the sky was falling to earth. Just like the others, Goosey-Loosey and Gander-Lander had no idea where to go, but they did not think of that. They ran on until they came to another field, where they met Turkey-Lurkey. He was very surprised to see them.

"My goodness, Chicken-Licken," he said, "why are you all so far from home and why do you look so worried?"

"A piece of the sky came down upon my head!" cried Chicken-Licken. "We are going to tell the king about it!"

"How terrible!" said Turkey-Lurkey. "Let me come with you!"

So Chicken-Licken, Henny-Penny, Cocky-Locky, Ducky-Lucky, Drakey-Lakey, Goosey-Loosey, Gander-Lander and Turkey-Lurkey scurried off to tell the king that the sky was falling to earth.

Turkey-Lurkey had just a little more sense than the other birds. He was the very first of them to stop and ask,

"But where does the king live?"

The other birds all stopped running and thought about this.

"This way," said Chicken-Licken and Henny-Penny, pointing to the east.

"No, this way," said Ducky-Lucky, pointing to the west.

Nobody could decide which way to go to find the king. They argued and argued.

And so it was that Chicken-Licken, Henny-Penny, Cocky-Locky, Ducky-Lucky, Drakey-Lakey, Goosey-Loosey, Gander-Lander and Turkey-Lurkey ended up running round and round in circles. They were still running round in circles when Foxy-Loxy came up to them with a sly smile upon his face. He was very pleased to see them.

"My goodness, Chicken-Licken," he said, "it is very brave of you to wander so far from home! How nice to see you! But what brings you here?"

"A piece of sky came down upon my head!" cried Chicken-Licken. "We were going to tell the king about it, but now we do not know where to go!"

The smile on Foxy-Loxy's face grew bigger and even more sly.

"Why, Chicken-Licken, you are fortunate indeed to have met me," he said, "for it just so happens that I know where the king lives. If you would all like to follow me I can take you there!"

"Oh, how kind!" said Chicken-Licken. "Thank you, Foxy-Loxy!"

So Chicken-Licken, Henny-Penny, Cocky-Locky, Ducky-Lucky, Goosey-Loosey, Gander-Lander and Turkey-Lurkey all scurried off together, following Foxy-Loxy, to tell the king that the sky was falling to earth.

Foxy-Loxy's smile was even bigger! He licked his lips.

He led the foolish birds right up to his lair.

"This way to see the king," he said and he stood back as Chicken-Licken, Henny-Penny, Cocky-Locky, Ducky-Lucky, Drakey-Lakey, Goosey-Loosey, Gander-Lander and Turkey-Lurkey all walked right inside. Foxy-Loxy had a wife and five little fox cubs, who were very hungry. In no time at all they had eaten Chicken-Licken, Henny-Penny, Cocky-Locky, Ducky-Lucky, Drakey-Lakey, Goosey-Loosey, Gander-Lander and Turkey-Lurkey. They spat out the feathers and crunched up the bones.

"That was delicious!" said Foxy-Loxy.

Poor Chicken-Licken never got to see the king to tell him that the sky was falling to earth.

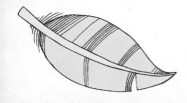